JoJo Siwa: 2018
A CENTUM BOOK 978-1-911460-74-9
Published in Great Britain by Centum Books Ltd
This edition published 2017
1 3 5 7 9 10 8 6 4 2

Centum Books Ltd, 20 Devon Square,
Newton Abbot, Devon, TQ12 2HR, UK
books@centumbooksltd.co.uk
CENTUM BOOKS Limited Reg. No. 07641486
A CIP catalogue record for this book is
available from the British Library
Printed in China

Contents

There's so much fun inside, including:

BE You

Super Cute

6

DREAM
Crazy
BIG

7

All about me

Fill these pages with all the cute, cool and crazy things about you and your life.

name: ....

nickname: ....

birthday: ....

age: ....

year born: ....

star sign: ....

home town/city: ....

BFF: ....

pets: ....

SWEET

Most embarrassing moment EVER:

....

....

....

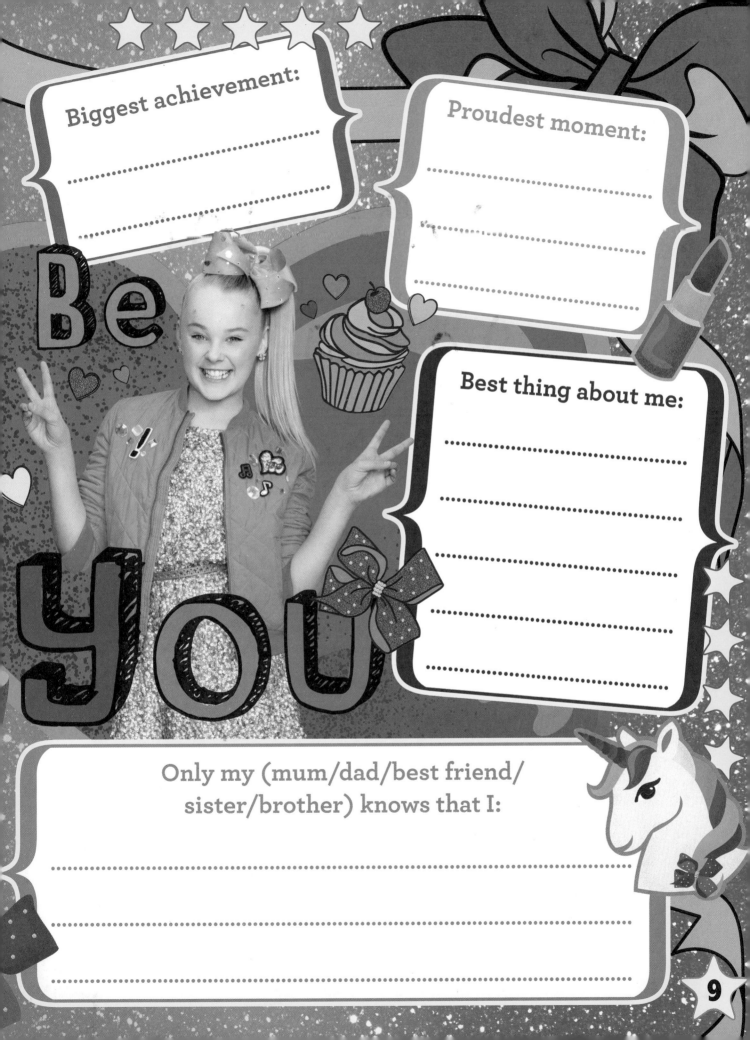

Biggest achievement:

....
....

Proudest moment:

....
....
....

Best thing about me:

....
....
....
....

Only my (mum/dad/best friend/
sister/brother) knows that I:

....
....
....

Be
YOU

9

Fave things

Fill this page with all your fave things.

friend: angeJdnr

family member: ar e550

movie: angew hedabar

TV show: n

vlogger:

choccy bar:

song:

shop:

animal:

sport:

food:

drink:

time of year:

day of the week:

The thing I love doing most in the world is:

....

....

....

DID YOU KNOW
JOJO'S FAVOURITE
DESSERT IS SHAVED ICE?

The first thing I do after I get up is:

....

....

....

....

The best part of the day is when I:

....

....

The last thing I do before I go to sleep is:

....

....

....

My life

★★★★	morning	afternoon	evening
Monday			
Tuesday			
Wednesday			
Thursday			
Friday			
Saturday			
Sunday			

Wake up at:

School starts at:

Eat lunch at:

Finish school:

Eat dinner at:

Go to sleep at:

DID YOU KNOW JOJO'S FAVOURITE SUBJECT IS MATHS?!

EAT DANCE SLEEP

13

Family tree

Fill in your family tree with names, pics or doodles to show who's who in your family.

Who is the cuddliest:
.... 3 eo ....

Who is the loudest:
Soolglb
....

me

me

Who is the happiest:
ame
....

Who is the messiest:
me
....

Who is the funniest:
me
....

me

Who is the chattiest:
me
....

georgia

Who is the cutest:
georl i a and me
....

Daddy

SWEET

Who is the smartest:
Daddy
....

BFF's

Which of your pals is your
best mate: evie

kindest pal: Kaiom

funniest friend:
James

oldest friend: Lilly

Which of your friends is the best dancer: Harrison

most organised: Isla

best shopper: E10

most scatterbrained: me

WHO IS MOST LIKE JOJO IN YOUR FRIENDSHIP GROUP?

BFF gallery

18

JOJO LOVES HER PET DOG BOWBOW. CAN DOGS BE BFFS? DEFINITELY!

19

Animal cuties

JoJo loves her cute dog BowBow! Number the animals on these pages from 1 to 20, with 1 for the most cute and 20 for the least.

Panda 1

Elephant 1

Piglet 16

Duckling 15

Kitten 13

Puppy 14

20

Mouse 15

Owl 11

Squirrel 12

Chick 2

Whale 10

Shark 9

Ladybird

Bumblebee 3

Monkey 8

Worm 18   18

Seal 4

Hedgehog 7

Goldfish 13

Parrot 6

21

Cutie cut-outs

Cut out all the cute pics on the following pages and use them to decorate your notebook, diary, bedroom or school locker.

BOWS MAKE EVERYTHING BETTER

This book belongs to:

This book belongs to:

This book belongs to:

This book belongs to:

This book belongs to:

This book belongs to:

TOP SECRET!

TOP SECRET!

TOP SECRET!

I ♥ my BFF

I ♥ my BFF

I ♥ my BFF

DO NOT DISTURB

DO NOT DISTURB

DO NOT DISTURB

Chill Out!

Chill Out!

Chill Out!

BE You

BE You

BE You

Sweet tweets!

Check out these JoJo-inspired hashtags, then write your own below.

#BestiesNotBullies
#PeaceOutHaterz
#BeYourSelfie
#ICanMakeYouDance
#JoJosJuice

....

....

....

....

....

....

....

....

....

....

Vlog it?

1.

Vlog idea:...

Main points to talk about:...

....

Props needed:...

2.

Vlog idea:...

Main points to talk about:...

....

Props needed:...

3.

Vlog idea:...

Main points to talk about:...

....

Props needed:...

28

4.

Vlog idea:...

Main points to talk about:...

....

Props needed:..

5.

Vlog idea:...

Main points to talk about:...

....

Props needed:..

DID YOU KNOW
THAT JOJO ENDS EVERY
VLOG BY THROWING
JUICE OVER HER HEAD?
THAT'S WHY HER CHANNEL
IS CALLED JOJO'S JUICE.

Closet cool

What does your dream closet look like? Draw it below and organise your clothes and accessories!

DID YOU SEE JOJO'S CLOSET TOUR VLOG? #GOALS

Will you organise by colour or type?

Fave foods!

List all your favourite foods on this page! Who would you invite to your dream dinner party? (JoJo, of course!)

Favourite fruits: ....banrna..

....

Favourite vegetables: ....cart..

....

Lunchbox essentials: ....cookys..

....

Favourite snacks: ....cookys..

....

Favourite international foods: ....pissa............................

....

Foods I want to try:...........se llry...

Favourite foods to share: ....

DID YOU KNOW JOJO LOVES CHICKEN WINGS?
SHE HATES HAMBURGERS AND HOT DOGS.

DREAM Crazy BIG

JoJo has always tried to follow her dreams and achieve her goals! She tells everyone to dream, crazy, big! In this section write down your hopes and dreams for the future.

WHY NOT TAPE THIS SECTION

TOGETHER, THEN OPEN IT UP AGAIN

IN THE FUTURE AND DISCOVER

IF YOUR DREAMS CAME TRUE?

Daydreamer

school

clothes

friends

holidays

celebs

food

ghosts

TV shows

movies

dancing

family

pets

34

Dream home

My dream home would be a:

mansion ♡
castle ♡
city flat ♡
ranch ♡
farm ♡
yacht ♡
caravan ♡
beach house ♡

My dream home would be:

next door to my BFF ♡
around the corner from where I live now ♡
up a mountain ♡
on a beach ♡
on a lake ♡
next to a river ♡
in a forest ♡
in the countryside ♡

Doodle your fave daydream in this bubble.

My dream home would be in:

UK ♡
Europe ♡
Asia ♡
Australia ♡
North America ♡
South America ♡
Africa ♡
Antarctica ♡
Arctic ♡

Dream holiday

What would your dream holiday be like?

My dream holiday would be in:

UK ♡

Europe ♡

Asia ♡

Australia ♡

North America ♡

South America ♡

Africa ♡

Antarctica ♡

Arctic ♡

I would travel by:

bike ♡

boat ♡

plane ♡

helicopter ♡

car ♡

submarine ♡

I would stay in a:

hotel ♡

caravan ♡

apartment ♡

castle ♡

I would eat:

fruit ♡

pizza ♡

ice cream ♡

sweets ♡

Dream job

What would your dream job be?

I would love to work with:

animals ♡

children ♡

only my friends ♡

on my own ♡

I would love to work:

in an office ♡

in a dance studio ♡

on the beach ♡

in a garden ♡

in a shop ♡

in a vehicle ♡

in a foreign country ♡

in space ♡

in the jungle ♡

Number these jobs from 1 to 12, with 1 being the one you'd most like to do and 12 the least.

vet

astronaut

teacher

TV presenter

doctor

vlogger

dancer

actor

engineer

marine biologist

firefighter

pilot

37

Decode your dreams!

Ever wondered what your dreams mean? Write about the last dream you remember below. Was it weird, crazy, scary, exciting or fun?

If you dream you are FALLING from the sky, down a hole or off a cliff, it can mean you feel out of control. Try to work out what area of your life you need to take control of, and what you can do about it.

If you dream you are FLYING, it means you feel confident and secure about your life and in control. If you dream you are flying too high, it can mean you are concerned how your success might change your life.

If you dream you are BEING CHASED, it means you have a problem in your life that you need to face up to and deal with.

WHATEVER YOUR DREAMS MIGHT MEAN, JUST REMEMBER TO DREAM BIG, JUST LIKE JOJO!

Rule the school!

Fill this page with all your fave things about your school!

name of your school:

....

fave subject:.......................................

fave teacher: ....

most amazing thing you've learned this year: ....

....

....

....

Number these subjects from 1 to 9, with 1 your most fave subject and 9 your least.

English

Science

Drama

Maths

Geography

PE

History

Music

Art

Technology

Use the space above to design a super-cute school uniform.

DON'T FORGET YOUR SCHOOL BAG!

41

Happy holidays

camping

beach

sightseeing

safari

activity

diving

skiing

cooking

horse riding

cruise

cycling

Other:

....

....

....

....

....

42

Best holiday memory ever:

....

....

If I could go on holiday with anyone, I would go with:

....

....

Worst holiday memory ever:

....

....

Name three places you have been to on holiday:

....

....

....

Name three places you would love to go on holiday:

....

....

....

Get ready for your next holiday with your top 5 items to pack:

....

....

....

....

Design your own cute suitcase to take on your next holiday.

43

Create your own blog

Use the spaces on these pages to plan your own blog or website, just like JoJo's.

Step 1

Think of a name or handle for your site:

www...

@ ....

Step 2

Design a logo and your masthead (the picture at the top of your site):

Step 3 — What kind of things would you blog about?

fashion

books

politics

art

friends

animals

news

movies

music

travel

other:
....

TV shows

Step 4

Decide how often will you post?

every day ♡

once a week ♡

once a month ♡

DON'T FORGET TO ALWAYS ASK A GROWN-UP BEFORE YOU GO ONLINE!

Step 5

Make sure you include popular hashtags to help share your content:

#..

#..

#..

Step 6

Decide who you will share your blog with and ask them to give you a mark out of 10.

family ♡

friends ♡

teachers ♡

Fashion haul

Which of the items below do want to add to your wardrobe?

If you did a JoJo-inspired fashion haul, which clothes would be on your fashion hit list? Create your dream haul on these pages.

- jeans
- dress
- maxi skirt
- trousers
- shorts
- mini skirt
- skirt
- T-shirt
- culottes
- jumper
- jacket
- waistcoat
- dungarees
- leggings
- hat

Tick all the colours you love to wear:

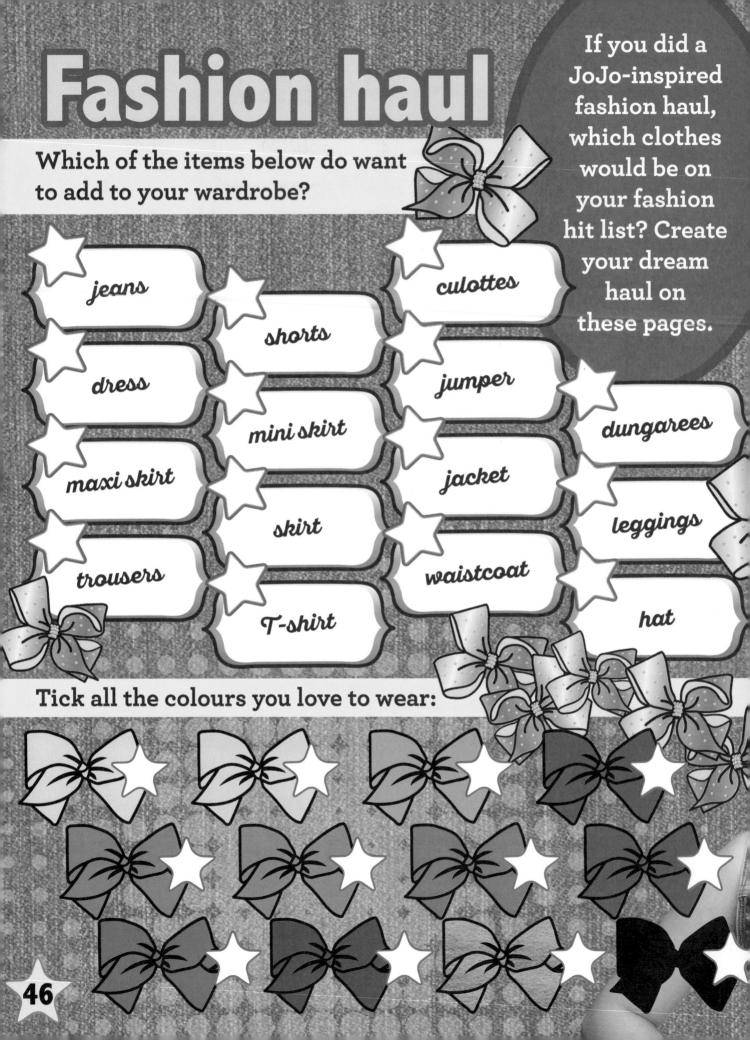

Where do you like to shop for...?

something fancy:

....

chill-out clothes:

....

sportswear:

....

accessories:

....

something different:

....

DID YOU KNOW JOJO'S FAVOURITE COLOUR IS GLITTER!

Design your dream outfit in this box:

JOJO HAS HER OWN UNIQUE SENSE OF STYLE! HOW WOULD YOU DESCRIBE YOURS?

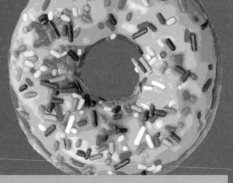

My routine

Fill out the chart to discover more about your routine. How often do you do the following?

	every day	twice a day	once a week	twice a week	once a month	never
wash your hair		✓				
brush your hair	✓					
brush your teeth	✓					
get a haircut					✓	
paint your nails					✓	
take a selfie					✓	
hang with your BFF					✓	
watch TV	✓					
play a video game						✓
go for a walk			✓			
do exercise					✓	
learn a new fact	✓					
dream about the future						✓

What are your good habits?

....
....
....
....
....

JOJO PRACTISES DANCE ROUTINES MOST DAYS A WEEK!

EAT DANCE SLEEP

Do you have any bad habits?

....
....
....
....
....

Copy draw

Copy and draw the cute pics on to the grids on these pages.

Colouring competition

Colour all the cute stuff on these pages. Ask each of your friends to colour in something, then pick your favourite!

From My Heart To Yours

Party fun

JOJO LOVES PARTIES – ESPECIALLY IF THERE'S DANCING INVOLVED AND LOTS AND LOTS OF GLITTER!

Birthdays are the best, right?! Even if your next one isn't till next year, it's never too early to start planning a party!

Step 1

Make a party invite list:

....

....

....

....

....

....

....

....

....

Step 2

Create a present wish list:

....

....

....

Step 3

Decide on a party theme:

pizza	♡	sleepover	♡
bowling	♡	swimming	♡
dance	♡	baking	♡
karaoke	♡	cinema	♡
beauty	♡		

CHECK OUT THESE COOL INVITES!

54

Continued on page 59.

....

IS HAVING A PARTY AND
WOULD LOVE YOU TO COME!

WHEN: ....
WHERE: ....
....
TIME: ....
RSVP: ....

....

IS HAVING A PARTY AND
WOULD LOVE YOU TO COME!

WHEN: ....
WHERE: ....
....
TIME: ....
RSVP: ....

....

IS HAVING A PARTY AND
WOULD LOVE YOU TO COME!

WHEN: ....
WHERE: ....
....
TIME: ....
RSVP: ....

....

IS HAVING A PARTY AND
WOULD LOVE YOU TO COME!

WHEN: ....
WHERE: ....
....
TIME: ....
RSVP: ....

Invite

To:

JoJo Siwa™

© Viacom

Invite

To:

JoJo Siwa™

© Viacom

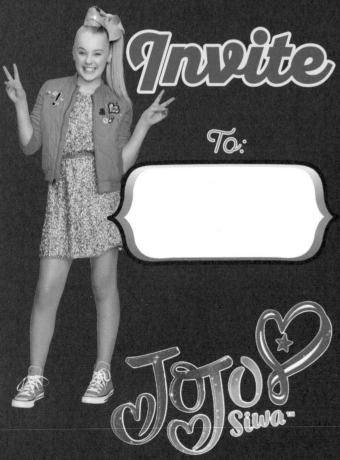

Invite

To:

JoJo Siwa™

© Viacom

Invite

To:

JoJo Siwa™

© Viacom

....

IS HAVING A PARTY AND
WOULD LOVE YOU TO COME!

WHEN: ....
WHERE: ....
....
TIME: ....
RSVP: ....

....

IS HAVING A PARTY AND
WOULD LOVE YOU TO COME!

WHEN: ....
WHERE: ....
....
TIME: ....
RSVP: ....

....

IS HAVING A PARTY AND
WOULD LOVE YOU TO COME!

WHEN: ....
WHERE: ....
....
TIME: ....
RSVP: ....

....

IS HAVING A PARTY AND
WOULD LOVE YOU TO COME!

WHEN: ....
WHERE: ....
....
TIME: ....
RSVP: ....

Invite

To:

Invite

To:

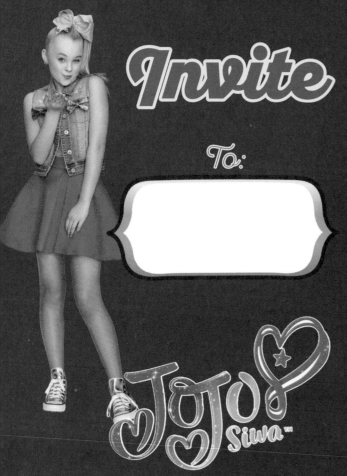

Invite

To:

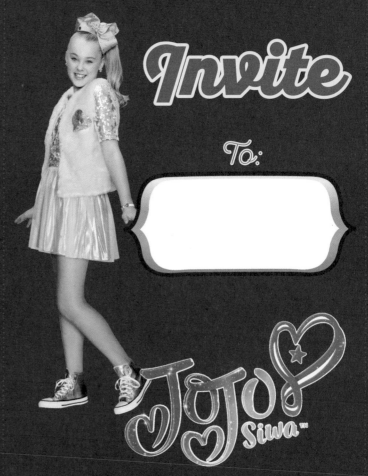

Invite

To:

Continued from page 54.

Step 4

What time will the party start and end?

Start:

Finish:

Step 5

Design the perfect party outfit below.

Bow designer

JoJo has so many bows because

BOWS ARE EVERYTHING!

Design JoJo a new bow on the template below, then design one for yourself on the page opposite.

60

BOWS ARE MY SUPER POWER

DID YOU KNOW JOJO HAS NEARLY 1,000 BOWS?! WHOA!